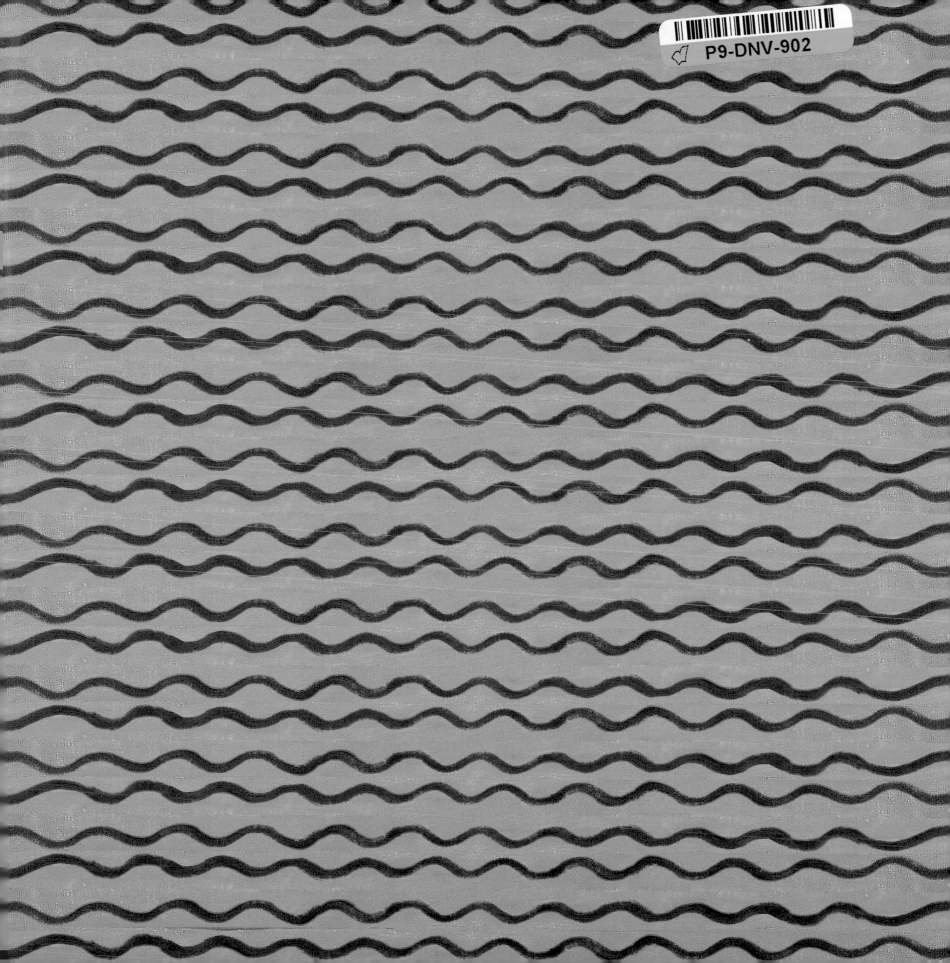

To my parents, Pedro and Mercedes, whose courage
inspired this story. –HCM

For all the Mexicans far from home.
Para todos los Mexicanos lejos de sus hogares. –LC

Library of Congress Cataloging-in-Publication Data

Martín, Hugo C., 1965–
  Pablo's Christmas / Hugo C. Martín ; illustrated by Lee Chapman.
      p. cm.
  Summary: When his father goes to America to find a job that pays more than toy making, young
Pablo has to act as the man of the house, protecting their small farm and trying to keep his mother
and sisters from worrying.
  ISBN-13: 978-1-4027-2560-9
  ISBN-10: 1-4027-2560-4
  [1. Farm life—Mexico—Fiction. 2. Fathers and sons—Fiction. 3. Christmas—Fiction. 4. Mexico—
Fiction.] I. Chapman, Lee, ill. II. Title.

PZ7.M363163Pab 2006
[E]—dc22

                                                                                           2005034457

1 2 3 4 5 6 7 8 9 10

Published by Sterling Publishing Co., Inc.
387 Park Avenue South, New York, NY 10016
Text © 2006 by Hugo C. Martín
Illustrations © 2006 by Lee Chapman
Designed by Randall Heath
Distributed in Canada by Sterling Publishing
C/o Canadian Manda Group, 165 Dufferin Street,
Toronto, Ontario, Canada M6K 3H6
Distributed in the United Kingdom by GMC Distribution Services
Castle Place, 166 High Street, Lewes, East Sussex, England BN7 1XU
Distributed in Australia by Capricorn Link (Australia) Pty. Ltd.
P.O. Box 704, Windsor, NSW 2756, Australia

Printed in China
All rights reserved

Sterling ISBN-13: 978-1-4027-2560-9
        ISBN-10: 1-4027-2560-4

For information about custom editions, special sales, premium and
corporate purchases, please contact Sterling Special Sales
Department at 800-805-5489 or specialsales@sterlingpub.com.

PABLO'S CHRISTMAS

BY
HUGO C. MARTÍN

ILLUSTRATED BY
LEE CHAPMAN

Sterling Publishing Co., Inc.

New York

On a small, dusty farm in Mexico, in the Valle de Guadalupe, a young boy named Pablo lived with his mother, father, and two little sisters, Isabella and Teresa.

Pablo's father was a talented wood-carver who had a joyful laugh, deep brown eyes, and a pair of hands that were knotted like strands of dark rope. But with those old hands he created beautiful toys and dolls, which he sold in the nearby town of Tepatitlán.

Life on the farm was not easy. Pablo spent every day hard at work, helping tend to the chickens, pigs, and goats the family raised on their tiny plot of rocky land.

Still, Pablo and his family were happy. At night after all the animals were fed, Pablo and his sisters sat on their creaky porch, listening to Papa tell Mexican folktales about the dark Madonna, an imprisoned princess, and a boy who tricked the devil.

One morning, as the family got ready to eat, Pablo's mother announced that she was going to have a baby. Pablo's father was happy but also secretly worried that the money he earned making toys would no longer be enough to feed his growing family.

As the sun began to set, he took Pablo for a walk by the dark woods near the house.

"Pablito, I have to tell you something," his father said.

"I need to go away with your uncle to America for a while to find work."

"But Papa, you have work here already. You are a wood-carver."

"Yes, but that brings in very little money, and soon we will have another baby to feed," said Papa. "In America, I will earn lots of money to bring home."

"Who will take care of us?" asked Pablo, his eyes wide, his stomach suddenly feeling scared and sick.

"You will have to be the man of the family while I'm gone. You can do it, Pablo," his father said. "I know you can."

It was summer, and Papa promised he would be home by Christmas. As he prepared to leave, Mama put on a brave face, but deep inside her heart was aching. "Remember, Pablo, I want you to be strong," Papa said. Then he began the long walk into town to catch a rickety bus to the border.

That night on the front porch, Pablo's mother tried to entertain the children with the old folktales, but she choked on the words. "Let me finish the story, Mama," Pablo said gently. He recounted the tales the family loved so dearly, until it was time for bed.

The summer days without Papa crept slowly by. Pablo tried hard to help his mother tend the farm. Pablo's sisters often worried about their father. Isabella told Pablo she was afraid that Papa had been tricked by a magical queen to fall in love and stay in America.

"Maybe he won't come back to us," Teresa agreed.

Pablo couldn't hear any more sad stories about his father, and went for a walk in the woods nearby. But he had never been through the woods alone. The trees seemed taller and the shadows more frightening.

Near a cave, Pablo suddenly felt he was being watched. He reached down and picked up a branch just as he saw two sets of eyes peering at him.

Coyotes.

Pablo felt his heart race as he held tightly to the branch and ran back home. Not wanting to frighten his sisters, Pablo told no one about the coyotes. Still, it took a while before he could catch his breath.

Once on the front porch, Pablo took out his father's special carving knife and began to whittle away at the branch. But the wood was very hard, and Pablo struggled just to cut away a tiny sliver.

At this pace, he would never become a wood-carver like his father. Pablo was frustrated but he kept whittling, even after his hands grew tight and cramped.

As winter approached and the shadows lengthened, life on the farm grew harder. The nights were colder and the food the family had stored away was fast running out. One day, things took a turn for the worse—coyotes snuck into the henhouse and ate two of the family's hens. Pablo's sisters cried, for they loved the hens very much.

"Don't worry, *hermanitas*," Pablo told the girls. "I won't let those coyotes get any more hens."

A few nights later, Pablo awoke from a deep sleep by the sound of squawking chickens. *The coyotes have returned!* he thought. Forgetting his fear, Pablo grabbed a broom and dashed into the henhouse, where two coyotes had cornered the fattest hen.

"*Vaya!* Go away, coyotes!" Pablo yelled, swinging the broom in the air.

The coyotes eyed Pablo for a few seconds and, seeing that he would not back down, scurried away through a hole in the back of the henhouse.

The coyotes were gone for now, but Pablo knew they would return.

Christmas was near and the happiness Pablo usually felt this time of year was replaced by sadness. He had no money for gifts, but he vowed to make it a good Christmas.

On Christmas Eve, the family ate warm *pozole* and *tortillas* and then cuddled around the fireplace.

"Everyone, close your eyes," announced Pablo, as he raced outside. He returned shortly, bringing with him a surprise.

"Open your eyes!" he shouted, hoping to get his mother and sisters in the holiday spirit. "It's our Christmas tree!"

"It's just beautiful," his mother said.

"But the tree has no decorations and we have no gifts to put under it," Isabella cried.

"Sure we do," said Pablo, pointing to two tiny, wrapped bundles under the tree. "And for decorations, I thought we could make popcorn with this dry maize and string it on the tree," Pablo said.

"Great idea, *hijo*," his mother exclaimed.

Mother pulled out her sewing needle and string and the girls began happily popping popcorn and stringing it around the tree. But just as the festivities were getting started, a terrible ruckus arose outside. It was the sound of scuffling and scratching at the door.

"The coyotes," said Pablo, jumping to his feet. "They've come back."

He reached for the broom and headed for the door.

"Stay inside, Pablo!" his mother cried.

"The coyotes are not going to ruin our Christmas," he shouted, preparing to fight for his family and home.

Suddenly, the door burst open, and a tall bulky figure appeared.

"FELIZ NAVIDAD!"

the figure shouted.

"Papi?" Teresa said.

"I told you I'd be back by Christmas," he said, holding a massive sack of gifts in his arms. There were toys, a new red dress for Mama, and candy for everyone.

"But Papa, you didn't bring any dolls back?" asked Isabella, peeking through the sack.

"I'm sorry—" Papa started. But Pablo interrupted.

"Don't forget to look under the tree!"

The girls dashed to grab the bundles. Giggling with delight, they tore off the wrapping to reveal two dolls that Pablo had carved.

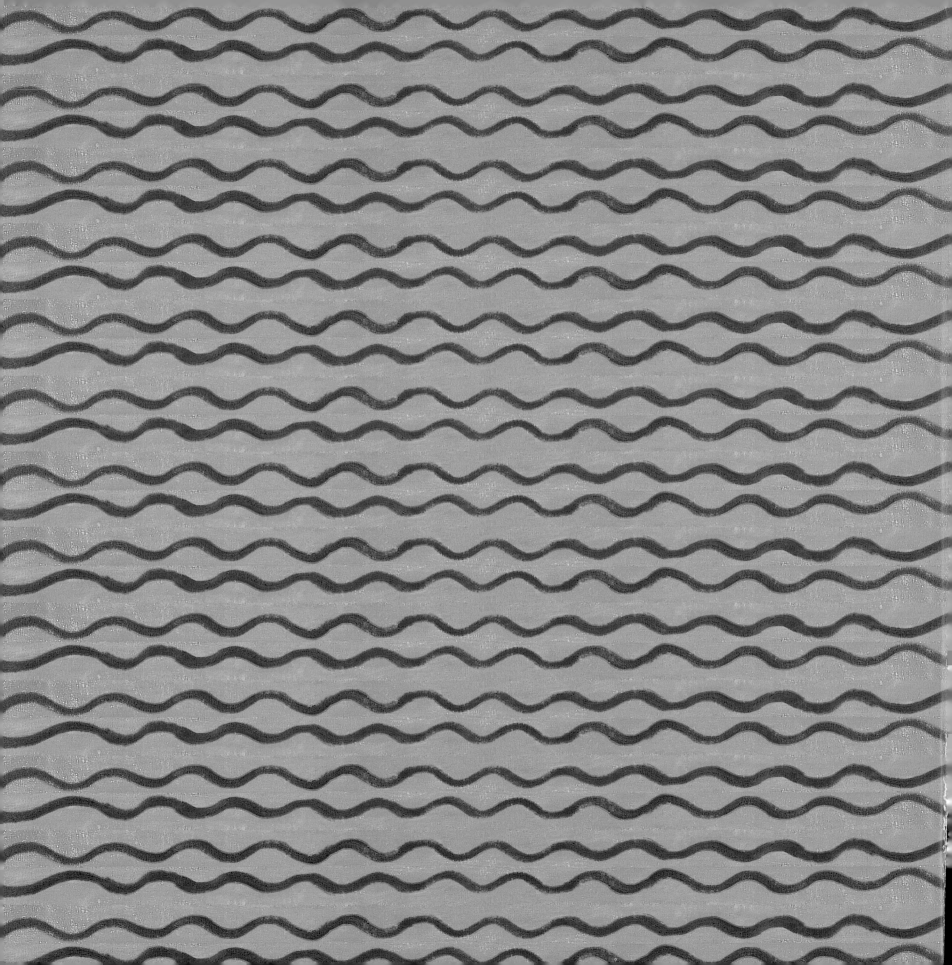